Sea Chest in the Attic

Warren H. Barton

Sea Chest in the Attic

by Warren Hussey Bouton

Illustrated by Barbara Kauffmann Locke

Hither Creek Press
Short Hills, New Jersey

First Paperback Edition, 2000

The characters and events in this book are ficticious. Any similarity to real persons, living or dead, is coincidental and not intended by the author.

ISBN 0-9700555-0-1

Printed in the United States of America

To Brenda, Sarah and Ben
Bob and Martha

And to the memory of
Reggie and Louise
Warren and Marjorie

Special thanks to
Barbara, Alex and Mary

CHAPTER 1

It was a great day to sail to Nantucket. The *Eagle* was a huge ship that could ferry more than 60 cars and hundreds of passengers from Cape Cod to the island. To me, a 12-year-old, it felt huge because there were three decks for people to wander around during the two-hour cruise. A lot of people were enjoying the ocean views and soaking up the summer sun outside on the top deck. I spent the time looking for my 8-year-old brother, Ben. He just couldn't sit still. One minute he was at the snack bar overloading on sugar and the next he was seeing how fast he could run from one end of the boat to the other.

I hadn't seen him for over half an hour when finally I spotted him looking over the rail in the bow.

"There you are! What are you up to now?" I asked.

"Why do you want to know, nosey old Sarah!? Are you writing a book? Just because you're my big sister doesn't mean I have to tell you what I've been doing! Mom and Dad may have put you in charge for the boat trip, but that doesn't mean I'm not allowed to have some privacy!"

This was the first time that Ben and I had been on the boat to Nantucket by ourselves. Mom and Dad had given us a hug on the dock and watched us walk up the gangplank and then we were off for a two-week adventure with Grandma and Grandpa on the island. The idea of the trip seemed exciting when we first planned it. But now, the realization that I would have to spend 14 days up close and personal with my brother made me wonder if it was such a good idea after all.

"I'm counting jellyfish!" Ben suddenly offered.

"Counting jellyfish? Yeah right! How many have you counted in the last half-hour? A dozen, two?"

"Five hundred and sixty-two! Is that enough for you?"

"You're kidding!" I quickly looked over the side and there were big, gross, ugly jellyfish all over the place. They weren't the clear kind that are hard to see but brownish, gushy things with tentacles that hung down in the water.

"Boy, I'd love to find one of those on the

beach. It'd be fun to stuff one in your face and watch you scream and run." Ben snickered.

Before I could come up with a good enough insult to throw back at my little brother, who through no fault of my own was also a child of my parents, someone behind us said, "Oh look, there's the island. I didn't think we were this close yet."

As Ben and I took our eyes off the water and the disgusting jellyfish, the island of Nantucket was before us. We could see the end of the jetties that lead into the harbor just a minute or two away. Off in the distance we could make out the steeple of the Congregational Church. There was the town clock, the water tower, and all the great houses up on the cliff. As we passed Jetties Beach there were boats everywhere. Windsurfers criss-

crossed in front of and behind our ferry, jumping the wake and having a great time. The *Eagle* slowly made its way around Brant Point Lighthouse and there were even more boats tied up to moorings. These were much bigger yachts from all over the world.

"Look, Ben, that one is from Australia!"

Ben shouted back, "Yeah, and that one has a helicopter on top. I want one of those!"

"Give me a break, Ben! Do you have any idea what they cost?"

"I don't care! When I'm an all-star pitcher in the major leagues I'll be able to buy whatever I want, and if I want a boat with a helicopter on top I'll buy one! Maybe I'll even buy two!"

As the *Eagle* pulled into the dock, we spotted Grandpa leaning up against his truck. Even though he was white-haired and just a little stooped, Grandpa was still a strong man. He loved doing odd jobs for people around the island and wherever he went he was usually followed by his little dog Rusty.

When we were close enough, the boat

crew quickly threw ropes to the men who work on the dock and before we knew it the passengers' gangplank was in place and we were ready to begin our great adventure on Nantucket. If Ben and I had known how terrifying this adventure was going to be, maybe we would have stayed on the boat!

CHAPTER 2

By the time we made it off the boat behind the crowds of people clamoring single-file down the gangway, Grandpa was on an intercept course to greet us.

"Hi, Grandpa!" I shouted.

"Do I know you?" he teased. "I'm here to meet my grandchildren, and they're quite a bit younger than you two. If somebody isn't here to meet you, I guess you'll have to walk wherever you're going!"

"Of course it's us, Grandpa! I'm Ben and that's Sarah! Don't you remember?" Ben didn't

always catch on when Grandpa was pulling his leg!

There was a twinkle in Grandpa's eye when he said, "Ben and Sarah? My grandkids are named that, too. Since they didn't show up, I think I might as well take the two of you home to Grandma and see if she notices the difference." With that he gave each of us a big hug and picked up the suitcases we were struggling to carry.

As we approached the truck, Rusty spotted us from his perch on the top of the seat. He quickly jumped into the back of the truck through the open rear window. He barked happily and wagged his tail as he spun around in circles.

"If you can fool Rusty, you'll be able to fool Grandma, too," Grandpa said with a smile.

"I guess I'll keep you. Let's put your suitcases in the back. Sarah, why don't you ride up front with me. Ben, you hop in back with Rusty. I'll try to give you a good bumpy ride over the cobblestones on Main Street!"

"All right! Drive as fast as you can, Grandpa! Jiggle my teeth loose!" Ben yelled.

The cobblestones were as jarring as ever. The only thing worse than driving fast on them in a truck was trying to navigate them on a bicycle. The street was rough, but the houses on either side were beautiful. Many big homes of brick or white clapboard had been built in the whaling days. Along the sidewalks were huge elm trees that must have been planted about the same time the houses were built. They were so tall they seemed to reach all the way to the sky. Main Street of Nantucket looked as if it came right out of a fairy tale. Before we knew it, that fairy tale was going to turn into a horror story!

Grandpa and Grandma's place was an old two story gray shingled house. It had been in the family for generations and had always felt just a little spooky to me. I don't know if it was the old furniture and the portraits of all my dead ancestors hanging around or the damp, musty smell of wood that never seemed to dry out because of the fog, but this was a house where I never wanted to be alone. Maybe the house scared me because it creaked at night and with all its nooks and crannies you could never be sure where the sounds were coming from. I always felt as if someone was just around the corner, watching, waiting.

When Mom had first talked about letting Ben and me come to the island by ourselves I had been really nervous about staying in Grandma and Grandpa's house. But I kept telling myself that it was all in my imagination. There was nothing there that could possibly hurt me, and besides, members of my family had lived there for years and nobody had ever even hinted that there was anything strange about the place. I had finally managed to put my fears aside. But now, as we pulled into the driveway, I began to have second thoughts.

CHAPTER
3

As soon as Grandpa stopped, Ben and Rusty jumped from the back of the truck and ran to the kitchen door. The screen slammed shut behind them before my feet even hit the driveway. "Hi, Grandma! What are you baking?" Ben yelled. "Smells like chocolate chip cookies. Fantastic!"

"Now be careful, you little scamp! They haven't cooled off yet. The chips will burn your tongue," Grandma scolded.

By the time Grandpa and I had the suitcases through the door Ben already had chocolate smeared in the corners of his mouth. In a matter of seconds he had single-handedly wiped out half a pan full of cookies.

"I hope there are some left for Sarah and me," Grandpa chuckled.

With that, Grandma looked up and a big smile filled her face. Oven mitts and all, she swept me up in a big hug.

"There's my favorite granddaughter," she cooed.

"Grandma, you always say that, but I'm your *only* granddaughter!"

"That's beside the point, dear. Whether I have one or a dozen, you're still special to me. Here, have a cookie. There's plenty more still to be baked."

Whenever our family visited Nantucket, Grandma always acted as if she had to feed us enough to last the entire year. There were always snacks and cookies around for us to nibble on. At mealtimes the table was loaded with enough food to feed an army. Sometimes Grandma even had to bring a serving table over because she ran out of room. Lunch and dinner were never over until dessert was served, and then before bedtime she would always ask if anybody wanted ice cream! And the answer was always yes! Ben was in seventh heaven whenever we visited with Grandma.

After the cookies were finished and we had spent some time sitting around the kitchen table catching up and telling about our trip on the boat, Grandma said, "Well, I tell you what. Why don't you take your things upstairs and get settled in. You'll both be in the back bedroom. Grandpa has started painting and papering the other two bedrooms up there, so you'll have to share until he's done with his project."

I couldn't believe it. My greatest fear was realized. I hated the back bedroom. It was down at the end of a long, dark, winding hall. The floor always creaked up there and, worst of all, in the corner of the back bedroom was a door that led into the attic. Not only that, but there was a window in that door to the attic. I didn't mind it during the day, but at night it always spooked me to think that if somebody or something was in the attic it could look out... and... watch me.

Ben's voice woke me from my panic. "I love the back bedroom! The attic has all kinds of neat, creepy things in it. I love to pretend that there are monsters hiding under the sheets! Do you still have that old sea chest, Grandma?"

"Yes, the sea chest is still there, Ben. Now scoot upstairs, settle in, and get cleaned up. It's almost time for dinner."

As we walked up the stairs, Ben was grinning. He was thrilled. But I was scared to death. Grandpa's project not only forced us to stay in the back bedroom but it meant my grandparents were sleeping downstairs in the guest room off the kitchen. Ben and I were going to be the only ones sleeping upstairs.

The floors creaked as Ben trotted toward our room. I followed him slowly. I just knew. I could feel in my bones that this wasn't going to be fun.

CHAPTER

4

Ben couldn't wait. By the time I had opened my suitcase he was calling to me through the open door of the attic.

"Sarah, come here! This place is great!"

The attic seemed to go on forever. There were old chairs and sofas and bureaus and other stuff covered with sheets. Boxes overflowed with books and papers. Portraits of more dead relatives leaned against posts holding up the roof.

As I made my way into the attic, I looked around at all the cobwebs and the dust. The thin light through the window at the end of the attic made everything seem scarier than it really was.

"Ben, where in the world are you?" I said shivering. "I can't see you. Why didn't you turn on the..." Suddenly, one of the sheets in the corner of the attic started to surge toward me. I couldn't move. My feet felt glued to the floor. I couldn't help it—I screamed at the top of my lungs. The sheet stopped right in front of me and before Ben burst into hysterical laughter, he whispered, "Boo!"

"I could kill you!" I screamed, once I had recovered from the shock. "What do you think you're doing, scaring me to death? I might have had a heart attack, a stroke, a nervous breakdown! That wasn't funny at all!"

"Oh, come on, Sarah. It was just a joke! There's nothing up here that could hurt you except maybe that old sea chest."

The sea chest was just the thing that I thought could hurt me. Ben had spotted it years ago. It was spooky. As long as we had been coming here it always made shivers run up and down my spine. The sea chest sat right in the middle of the attic. It was big enough to hide a body, and Ben claimed that there was probably a pirate's skeleton hidden inside. The strangest thing about the chest was the rhyme that was carved on the top.

> The Sea Chest's riddle can be solved by a
> book...
> It's easy to find if you know where to look.
> Tell me the ship where I was stored in the
> hold.
> Tell me my captain who was careless yet
> bold.
> How many tails were viewed on my trip?
> How many whales met their end by my ship?
> Do not open me unless you can answer...
> Or horrors untold will chase you hereafter.
> If you are foolish a great fog will loom...
> Without the right answers you'll surely be
> doomed.

"Sarah, Ben dear, it's time for dinner," Grandma called.

I was so thankful to get away from that old box I ran from the attic.

It wouldn't be the last time that I ran in terror from that horrible sea chest.

CHAPTER 5

Sunlight shining through the back bedroom window made me squint and cover my head with the bed sheet as I awoke the next morning. Somehow, I had managed to get the events of last night, Ben's joke, the sea chest, the attic window, and everything else out of my mind and gotten a decent night's sleep. The smell of fresh blueberry muffins drifted up the stairs from Grandma's kitchen. The wonderful aroma even woke Ben.

"What is that great smell? Have I died and gone to heaven?" he asked.

"Not yet—Grandma's baking again!" I

said as I stretched and got ready for a quick run downstairs. There was no sleeping late at Grandma's. Muffins, bacon, eggs, pancakes, and waffles with strawberries on top were all specialties of the house. But if you stayed in bed too long Grandma would say, "Sorry, the kitchen is closed. You missed your chance. Even the best hotels and restaurants only serve breakfast for so long! Get it while it's hot or get...it...not!"

After a fantastic breakfast of muffins and eggs, fried to perfection, Ben and I headed downtown to explore our favorite shops and to pick up a newspaper for Grandpa.

The day was bright and beautiful. The sky was an incredible Nantucket blue and there was just enough of a nip in the air to make us put on our sweatshirts. Every time we visited we just had to stop in at our favorite shops—the gift shop that used to be the home of a famous sea captain, the fudge shop, and, of course, the Hub. The Hub was like a giant newsstand with the latest magazines, books, and newspapers from all over the world.

Downtown was a madhouse of activity. It felt as if everyone on the island was out running errands early so they could spend the rest of the day at the beach. The farm trucks selling Nantucket-grown vegetables had lines of customers waiting for corn, tomatoes, and bouquets of flowers.

"Why would anybody wait in line for vegetables?" Ben wondered aloud as we squeezed past the mob.

I didn't bother responding because, after all, what sense would it make to try to convince an 8-year-old boy that there really was value to eating something besides pizza, hamburgers, and stuff made out of sugar!

Later as we headed home after our excursion, Ben suddenly asked, "Sarah, what do you think is really in that sea chest? I mean, do you think it's really cursed, or is it all a joke?"

"Ben, all I know is I don't want to have anything to do with it," I said. "I don't even want to talk about it. That thing makes my skin crawl. There's something strange about that box, something that feels evil. I've never felt anything like it in my life. I'm scared even to be sleeping in that bedroom."

"Oh come on. Don't be a wimp! You're still mad at me 'cause I teased you yesterday with the sheet."

"Yes, I am still mad about your stupid

joke, but that's not all. When I was in the attic yesterday, it felt as if my heart stopped beating. I couldn't move, and it wasn't just you and the sheet. The moment I screamed I looked away from you toward the box. At the very moment when I was the most terrified, that old sea chest started to gleam with an eerie blue glow. It was as if it was feeding off my fear." I shivered again. "I don't want to talk about it any more. Let's just pretend it never happened and go to the beach."

With that I started to run up the street so that Ben couldn't see the tears of fear that started running down my cheeks.

CHAPTER

6

As soon as I made it through the kitchen door, Grandma looked up from the sandwiches she was making and said, "Oh good, you're home! I hope Ben is right behind you, because Grandpa and I thought it would be best to head to the beach early and have our lunch there. I'm almost done putting things together, so why don't you run upstairs and get your bathing suit on. We'll be going out to Madaket, and if we're not there soon, we'll have to park all the way down at the boat landing!"

Whenever we hit the beach with Grandma and Grandpa, we always went to

Madaket. My great-grandfather had loved the peace and quiet of the west end of the island. In her teenage years, Grandma had spent a lot of time running through the sand dunes and enjoying the surf there. It was a lot more crowded now, but it was still a very special place for our family.

"Okay, Grandma, it won't take me long to change and grab my towel. I'll be ready before Ben even makes it through the door!"

By the time Ben was home and changed, Grandpa's truck was loaded with everything we needed for the beach. We had coolers stuffed with food and drinks. There were two beach umbrellas, towels, boogie boards for riding the surf, not to mention baseball gloves, books, sunglasses, and enough sunscreen to cover a whale. Grandma liked to be prepared!

The beach was terrific. It was wide with beautiful, clean sand, and the sun sparkled off the deep blue water. The surf was calm by most standards, but it was just right for me. One of my favorite things to do at the beach is to stand in the wash of the surf and look for pieces of quahog shells that have been broken and polished by the water and sand. Some of the pieces are colored purple. Many years ago, the Indians used the shells, which they called *wampum*, as money.

Once we had found our spot and set up all our stuff, the time just flew. There were so many ways to have fun. If we weren't riding the waves we were flying one of the kites we had brought along. When we got bored with that we'd walk along the beach toward the point and look for sand dollars. Of course we could always just sit, enjoy the view, or read the newest spine-tingler mystery. It was a great place to spend a day.

The afternoon wore on. Grandpa had wandered off toward the point with Rusty to see how the fishermen were doing and Grandma had started to gather things together to load back into the truck. Ben and I were just watching the waves when Ben suddenly asked, "Grandma, where did that old sea chest in the attic come from?"

As soon as he asked his dumb question I could feel my neck start to burn. Why did he have to bring that stupid thing up? He knew it scared me!

"That chest has been up there for years," Grandma answered. "In the old days there used to be a lot of shipwrecks because of the sandbars around Nantucket. When a ship went down or broke into pieces, a lot of the cargo would wash onto the beach and the islanders would pick things up and take them home. Waste not, want not! Your great-grandfather told me that sea chest came off an old whaling ship. The Nantucket whaling fleet sailed all over the world. There's no telling where it came from. Don't know why the family has kept it all these years. We've never been able to find a key to open it. By the sound of the rhyme on top, it's just as well! Of course that's all foolishness," Grandma laughed.

It wouldn't be long before we realized that the sea chest was nothing to laugh about!

CHAPTER
7

That night as I walked to our back bedroom after brushing my teeth, I saw to my horror that the attic door was open. As the panic started to swell up inside of me, I could hear Ben muttering to himself under his breath. When I finally gathered up the courage to look through the attic door, I saw him kneeling in front of the sea chest.

"There must be *some* way to get into this old thing," he sputtered. "Maybe I could pop it open with a screwdriver."

"Ben, no!" I screamed as I ran into the attic and stood behind him.

"I bet a knife would do it. I know, a crowbar..."

"Ben, please no!" I could hardly control myself. I tried to pull him away, but he was possessed by the idea that he had to get into that old box.

"Sarah, get used to it. I'm going to figure this out! Maybe there's treasure inside!"

"Ben, forget about it. There's nothing in there!" I pleaded.

"Okay, maybe there's nothing or, even worse, maybe there's something evil, but I have to find out!" he yelled. "It's driving me crazy!"

I started pulling at Ben. "Give it up! What you're doing is crazy. It's wrong! I know whatever is in that sea chest is horrible and wicked. We have to get out of here and just leave it alone."

I dragged Ben away from the chest. When we were finally back in our room, I slammed the door to the attic shut and cried, "Stay out of there! Leave it alone—that sea chest is evil!

Don't ever go into the attic again!" I was shaking so hard that even Ben started to feel frightened.

After I turned out the light, it was hours before I finally drifted off to sleep.

That night I dreamed about the attic. In my dream, the latch that held the attic door shut started to rattle and shake as if something on the other side wanted to burst into our room. There was also a spooky blue glow coming from that awful window in the attic door.

Maybe it wasn't just a dream.

CHAPTER
8

Days went by and Ben just couldn't get that sea chest out of his mind. He never mentioned it because he knew I would get hysterical again, but I could tell he was always thinking about the attic and that old box covered by cobwebs and dust. Sometimes he seemed so far away that even Grandma began to notice. When she asked him if he was okay he would just shake his head, scrunch his shoulders, and reply, "I'm fine, Grandma. Maybe I'm just a little homesick." But all the time he was really trying to decide the best way to break into that horrible thing. He was possessed!

One morning we woke up, not to the smell of Grandma's cooking but to the sound of rain beating against the bedroom window. It was the first day of our trip that the beautiful Nantucket blue sky was replaced by dark, ominous thunderclouds. When Ben and I made our way into the kitchen and sat down at the breakfast table, Grandma announced that the day had finally arrived for us to go to the Nantucket Whaling Museum! My heart sank. To me, that was a fate worse than death! With the exception of spending the day in the attic, I couldn't think of anything that could possibly be worse than a museum, any museum!

Once the breakfast dishes were done, Ben and I stalled as long as we could. We dillied. We dallied. We tried to convince Grandma that we wanted to spend the day reading, cleaning the house, even polishing the silver, but none of our excuses worked.

"Your family has a very proud history on this island," Grandma explained. "It's time you learned about it. People come from all over the world to do research in our fine museum. There's no reason why you shouldn't spend some time there and appreciate the history of this wonderful island. Your ancestors are important—if not to you, then to the rest of Nantucket and the world! I just can't understand why you don't want to bother yourselves to learn about them..."

By the time Grandma finished we knew we were going to the museum. There was no arguing with her once she got going about the family history. We were being led to the slaughter and we knew it!

The Whaling Museum was crowded because of the weather. Grandpa had delayed our expedition until after lunch by insisting that he needed Ben and me to help him with one of his projects. Once lunch was over, however, there was no sidetracking Grandma. "We're going to the museum if I have to carry you there myself!" she exclaimed.

The museum is a large brick building that used to be a candle factory at the height of the whaling days. The main floor is one big open room filled with harpoons, lances, ship's rigging, and a whaleboat that had been used to chase the unsuspecting mammals.

"How could people kill such beautiful animals, Grandma?" I asked. "They're intelligent and gentle. Why would anybody do that?"

Grandma responded slowly and with a lot

of thought. "It was a different time, Sarah. There were lots of whales back then and the oil that came from their bodies was used for all kinds of things. People didn't think of whales as intelligent, beautiful creatures. They were seen as a resource that was used to make people's lives better. I'm not saying it was right. But at the time they thought it was."

We moved on through the many rooms of the museum. In one there was a skeleton of a whale that had once washed up on the beach. It was huge! Other rooms were filled with paintings of Nantucket whaling captains, ivory carvings, and stuff brought back by sailors who had traveled the South Seas searching for whales.

The museum was turning out to be pretty interesting, but still, Ben and I were starting to get a little itchy when Grandma said, "Oh look, there's one more room left. Let's see what's there and then, since you've been so good, we can get some ice cream on the way home." With an offer like that we could certainly stand a few more minutes of Nantucket history.

As it turned out, the room was dedicated to the many shipwrecks around the island. In addition to maps locating the wrecks and pictures of ships being smashed by horrible waves, there was also an exhibit of things that had washed ashore. There were ships' wheels, giant barrels that had carried whale oil, and figureheads that were once proudly mounted on the front of great ships and now were stuck in a museum collecting dust. One display had a bunch of small stuff, including a captain's Bible, a logbook—a sort of diary in which the events of each day on the ship were recorded—and a number of other things.

I moved on, but Ben just kept staring at the display. He didn't budge. Grandma was getting ready to leave, but still Ben stood there, as if he were spellbound.

"What are you staring at?" I asked as I moved to his side. Then I looked at the exhibit again, and I spotted something I hadn't seen the first time. Right in the middle of the display was a strange old key.

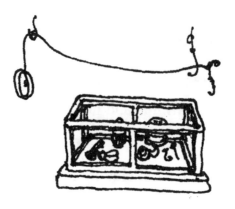

CHAPTER
9

"I have to have that key!" Ben whispered, never taking his eyes from the display. "I know it belongs to the sea chest in the attic. I can feel it!"

I knew exactly what he was thinking. "Ben, don't even think about stealing that key," I whispered. "It belongs to the museum. You'll get into trouble!"

"It belongs to me!" he muttered as he quickly grabbed the key from the exhibit and slipped it into his pocket.

"Ben, I'll tell on you and..." But before I

could finish Ben had grabbed both my arms and was looking straight into my eyes.

"No, you won't!" he growled in a low voice that suddenly sounded dangerous. "You won't say anything to anybody!"

His voice scared me to death. I'd never heard him sound so angry and almost evil. If that wasn't enough, as I looked into his face his lips turned into a sneer and there was the strangest blue glow coming from the whites of his eyes.

Grandma broke the spell between us as she suddenly came around a museum showcase saying, "Well, I guess this was a pretty good way for the two of you to pass a rainy day! What have you found that is so interesting? Oh, for heavens sake! These things came from the wreck of the whaleship *Joseph Starbuck*. I think that's the same wreck my great-grandfather told me the sea chest came from. Isn't that something? Now, let's go get that ice cream!"

As we walked down the street toward the ice cream shop, I can guarantee you that sweets were the last thing on my mind. Now I knew Ben would finally get his wish. He had the key that would open the sea chest. I could only hope that it was really empty and that the haunting riddle on the lid was someone's idea of a scary joke.

But somehow I knew that the strange verse was no joke.

CHAPTER
10

As soon as we got back to Grandma and Grandpa's house, Ben started to rush for the stairs. Before he made it through the dining room, Grandma called, "Now Ben, where do you think you're going? I could use some help setting the table for dinner, and there's corn that needs to be husked. You and Sarah get those things done and, when you're finished with those jobs, come and see me. I have a few more things you could do. After all, this morning you both wanted to help around the house. Now is a good time to start!"

I could tell Ben wasn't very happy and

that all he wanted to do was get up to the attic. But he also didn't want to make Grandma mad by disappearing when she'd asked him to help. He hurried through his jobs, but every time he finished one, Grandma gave him another.

Dinner seemed to last forever. I was glad because the last thing in the world I wanted was for Ben to find his way into the attic with the key he had stolen. He hardly said a word at the table. As Grandpa slipped a piece of his meal to Rusty, under the table, he asked with a grin, "So how was the tour? I bet it was just loads of fun! I can't think of a better place to spend an afternoon than the good old Whaling Museum!"

"It was fine," I answered. "Ben really liked the room dedicated to the shipwrecks around the island."

With that Grandma jumped in. "As a

matter of fact, Sarah and Ben were especially interested in an exhibit of things that washed ashore from the wreck of the whaleship *Joseph Starbuck*. It just so happens that the old sea chest up in the attic may have come from the same wreck. Isn't that a coincidence?"

Ben was becoming very uncomfortable with the conversation. Even though he wanted to get to the sea chest, he didn't want to be reminded that he'd stolen the key.

"Grandma, if it's okay, I think I'm going to head upstairs to our room. I'm really tired and my stomach isn't feeling too good," he finally said.

"If you don't want any dessert, you must not be feeling well." Grandma worried. "You head on up and just rest for a while. That ice cream before dinner must have done you in."

Before I could blink, Ben was gone. He ran up the stairs and, by the sound of things, he jumped both beds in our room and threw open the door to the attic.

"I think I'd better check on Ben," I said. "He was acting really funny this afternoon, and Mom asked me to watch out for him." Before Grandma could answer, I was halfway up the stairs myself. I knew where he'd be and I had to stop him if I could.

Ben was already kneeling in front of the sea chest. The key was in the lock and just as I shouted "No, Ben!" he twisted the key.

At first nothing happened. The lock didn't budge, but as he jiggled the key, I heard the tumblers of the lock release. The sea chest was unlocked. My brother looked into my eyes and, as a satisfied grin spread over his face, the lid slowly opened by itself. It was as if an invisible hand had taken control and the jaws of something horrible were opening to eat us alive.

When the sea chest was fully open, Ben and I got a surprise. The sea chest was...empty. I have never been so relieved in my life. All my worrying had been for nothing. Of course, Ben was disappointed. I've never seen him so frustrated and upset. All the figuring, the scheming, and stealing the key was for nothing. He just couldn't believe it was empty. You should have heard him! The words that came out of his mouth were not the kind that I would want to repeat. Ben was so angry that he tried to slam the lid shut, but each time he tried, the lid just slowly opened again all by itself. After a while he even tried to lock the chest again, but the key wouldn't move and the lid just popped open time and again.

"Come on, Ben," I said. "Let's just leave it for tomorrow. We can figure out how to close it when we're not so frustrated and tired. Let's just cover it up with one of these sheets and go to bed. There's nothing in there anyway. We'll take care of it in the morning."

"Okay, we'll lock it up tomorrow," Ben mumbled. "I never should have bothered with it in the first place. It was all a waste of energy. Stupid sea chest!" We shut the attic door behind us and got ready to hit the sack after a long, nerve-wracking day.

When the light was out and Ben and I had somehow drifted off to sleep, something frightful was happening in the attic. Little did I know it, but my worst nightmare was coming true. Beneath the sheet, a bluish light slowly crept from the open chest, giving the attic an eerie glow. Thin wisps of fog floated slowly out from under the edges of the sheet, filling the attic with a damp chill.

The riddle of the sea chest was coming true!

CHAPTER 11

The next day was stormy again. The wind blew from the northeast and the rain came down in buckets. This was not what we'd had in mind when we came to Nantucket—every day was supposed to be a beach day or at least dry enough for us to be outside and enjoying the island. But here we were, stuck in Grandma and Grandpa's old house. Of course, both Ben and I knew we needed to find a way to close that stupid sea chest, but since it was empty, the excitement and the fear had worn off. Now, getting it closed was just another job. We tried reading. We watched a little TV, but the only things that were on were dumb old talk shows and soap operas. We'd already been to the museum, and even though Grandma told us there were more "places of interest" to visit, we managed to convince her that one museum was about all we could handle.

Finally, when we were so bored we thought our heads would explode, I said to Ben, "Let's see if we can get the sea chest closed. There's nothing else to do."

Ben responded in a ho-hum voice, "Okay, let's get it over with."

We trudged up the stairs, down the hall, and through our room with all the excitement of a snail race, and opened the door to the attic.

Something was wrong! A blast of cold, clammy air hit us square in our faces. Fog had

filled the entire space. It was moving, swirling as if it were alive. Everything in the attic, from the paintings to the furniture, was almost invisible. As we moved into the attic to get a better look, the door slammed behind us and suddenly we saw a bright blue glow. It was coming from the sea chest!

Ben and I held onto each other as a strong, horrible voice bellowed from the chest: "Who is it dares disturb my sleep? Answer my riddle and your life you shall keep!"

My Sea Chest's riddle can be solved by a
    book...
It's easy to find if you know where to look.
Tell me the ship where I was stored in the
    hold.
Tell me my captain who was careless yet
    bold.
How many tails were viewed on my trip?
How many whales met their end by my ship

Do not open me unless you can answer...
Or horrors untold will chase you hereafter.
If you are foolish a great fog will loom...
Without the right answers you'll surely be
    doomed.

With every word that terrible voice said, the fog around us moved faster and faster. It seemed to grab at us, and as our fear grew so did the strength of that spooky blue light. "Do you know the answer to my rhyme or has your life's clock just run out of time?"

Ben and I panicked. Ben began to cry as a hand of fog wrapped around his leg and began pulling him toward the sea chest. I grabbed my little brother as I blurted out, "You're from the *Joseph Starbuck*. You were in the hold of the whaleship *Joseph Starbuck*!"

The fog let go of Ben and the light from the chest dimmed a little. But the voice was every bit as strong and haunting.

> The pretty girl is as smart as she looks.
> But the knowledge you have did not come
>   from a book.
> My captain, young child—what was his
>   name?
> Answer my riddle or your fate is the same!
> How many tails? How many whales?
> Answer me now or the fog will prevail!

"We don't know," I cried. "Leave us alone!

We didn't mean to bother you. We just wanted

to see what was in the chest."

The voice bellowed again:

> Curiosity, child, is little excuse.
> My riddle was clear and it's you I accuse.
> My fog it will come, my fog it will loom.
> All that you love will surely be doomed.

The voice then broke into a sickening laugh

as the fog seemed to reach out for us again. Ben

and I ran for the attic door. I reached it first and struggled with the latch, but it just wouldn't open. "Ben, help me! Help me! I can't get it open by myself," I screamed.

Ben grabbed the handle too, and with all our strength, we forced the latch open. We burst through into our bedroom and slammed the door behind us. But even as we held it shut, the blue light radiated through the attic window and wisps of fog seeped under the door. And that wasn't all. Without warning, the latch started to jiggle on its own, and we could hear the sound of horrifying laughter echo through the room.

CHAPTER 12

"We have to find the answers to the rhyme!" I shouted in Ben's ear as we struggled to keep the door closed.

"How can we find them?" Ben blubbered through his tears. "The fog's going to get us. It'll get Grandma and Grandpa and turn their house into mist."

"No, it won't! I won't let it!" I was starting to get angry. "Think! The answers are in a book. What book? Where could we find information about the whaleship *Joseph Starbuck*?"

"The museum!" Ben exclaimed. "The

display where I found the key had a logbook. The captain's name will be there, and so will the number of whales that were sighted and caught. We have to get to the museum!"

I knew Ben was right. He had to be right!

"On the count of three, run for it," I said. "There's no time to waste. We'll run straight to the Whaling Museum. If we have to take the logbook to get the answers, we'll take it. One, two, three, *go!*"

Ben and I scrambled over the beds and ran down the hall to the stairs. Our feet hardly touched the steps as we bounded down and out through the dining room. Grabbing our raincoats as we raced through the kitchen, we shouted at Grandma, "We're going to the museum!"

"But we were just there yesterday!" she said to the door swinging behind us.

"Hmmm...something must have really sparked their interest! Maybe there's hope yet for the younger generation!"

But while Grandma smiled with hope for the future, the door to the attic slowly opened and fog began to creep into the corners of our bedroom.

CHAPTER
13

I have never run so fast in all my life, and Ben was right beside me all the way. Through the rain, over the puddles, from street to street, we dashed until we finally reached the museum. It was only the solemn stares of the people who worked inside that slowed us down. There was no way we could run up the stairs to the shipwreck room without attracting too much attention. As we made our way to the display that held the answers to the riddle of the sea chest, we pretended to be calm and interested children. It also gave us a minute to catch our breath.

But our breathing stopped dead as we entered the room dedicated to the wrecks around Nantucket. The display where Ben had found the key was gone! In its space was a sign that read "THIS EXHIBIT HAS BEEN TEMPORARILY REMOVED. SORRY FOR THE INCONVENIENCE."

I couldn't believe it. My face went pale. My stomach turned and churned and I felt as if I was going to throw up. Ben didn't look any better. He just stared at the sign without saying a word.

"May I help you?" asked a deep voice behind us. Ben and I were so startled that we almost jumped out of our skin. When we turned, we were relieved to see a big man with friendly eyes, gray hair, and a warm smile. He was wearing a name tag that said "Reginald

Hussey," identifying him as someone who worked in the museum.

"I'm sorry if I frightened you, but it's not often that I find children of your age so interested in an empty display! It's too bad that the exhibit had to be removed, but we discovered yesterday afternoon that something had been stolen. The person in charge of the museum was afraid the thief might come back for something else, so we put things away for a little while."

That sinking feeling in my stomach just got stronger and stronger. How could we ever get the answers to the sea chest's riddle without the logbook? The fog would get us for sure. If we didn't get back to the attic soon, our bedroom and probably the house would be dissolved by the mist.

But I wasn't going to give up! Desperate situations call for desperate measures! And so with all the courage I could find I said, "As a matter of fact, Mr. Hussey, you can be of some help." As I spoke, Ben looked at me as if I was possessed. He'd never heard me sound so grown-up or smart! "We came to the museum today to do a little research." I continued calmly. "Our family has a...connection with the whaleship *Joseph Starbuck* and we had really hoped, with your help of course, to look at the logbook. It's quite important to us."

"That's a very serious request, young lady," Mr. Hussey replied thoughtfully. "But you two must be very interested, and I think that's wonderful. Come with me. I just happen to know where they put it!"

We followed our new friend through a

door that was marked "Museum Staff Only" and found ourselves in a storeroom filled with all kinds of stuff that must have had something to do with the island's history. A few things looked as if they might have come from whaling ships. Mr. Hussey moved around an old library table toward a giant walk-in safe built into the wall. He slowly opened the heavy unlocked door and disappeared inside for just a minute. When he came out, he was holding the thick logbook of the *Joseph Starbuck*, which he gently placed on the table where we could all see it.

Ben and I could hardly contain ourselves. We wanted to grab the book and run home, but we could tell there was no way to hurry Mr. Hussey.

"You have to be very careful with old books like this. The air dries them out and the

pages get brittle," he told us.

The leather of the cover creaked a bit as Mr. Hussey turned it back to reveal the first page, which read: *The logbook of the whaleship Joseph Starbuck as recorded by its captain, Ichabod Paddack.*

That was the first answer we needed. Ichabod Paddack was the captain who the riddle claimed was "careless yet bold." But how in the world could we find out how many tails and how many whales had been sighted and caught without looking at every single page? We'd be here all day if we had to do that. The house and maybe even Grandma and Grandpa would be gone!

"Mr. Hussey, Ben and I were wondering if there's any way to tell how many whales the crew spotted and how many they killed."

Turning the pages carefully, Mr. Hussey answered, "Well, let's see. The captain used a special stamp to keep track. Here, there's only half a whale—that means the lookout sighted one. And over here is a stamp of a whole whale. That means they caught it. We could just look through the book and add them all up... but I wonder though if there isn't a place in the back where they wrote down a total."

Slowly, Mr. Hussey turned to the back of the logbook. He was being so careful that Ben and I were ready to go crazy! Finally, he said, "Well, looky here! The crew of the *Starbuck* spotted 177 whales and harpooned 56."

That's all we needed to know! As soon as the words were out of Mr. Hussey's mouth, Ben and I ran for the door. As we rushed away, we called out "Thank you! Thank you! We need to get home!"

CHAPTER
14

We ran and ran and ran. The rain had stopped while we were in the museum, but we knew that inside the house the fog was rolling on and on, melting away everything it touched.

Grandma and Grandpa were sitting at the kitchen table sharing an afternoon snack when we burst through the door. We didn't even slow down long enough to grab a cookie. When we reached the bottom of the stairs, the fog was already blanketing them. It floated and swirled angrily, just as it had in the attic. One side of the stairs was almost invisible, and the other side was wet and slippery as if disintegrating with each wisp of fog. We grabbed hold of the railing and pulled ourselves up one step at a time. Both of us slipped every few steps, and once Ben almost fell down to the bottom, but finally we made it to the top.

The hallway was cold and clammy, and I could put my hand right through the walls. The floor was slimy, and everywhere the fog pulled and pressed us toward the attic door. There was no getting away this time. The blue light was stronger now. Even through the fog there was no mistaking its brilliance. It was feeding off the fog and our fear. Horrible laughter poured from the attic, and then we heard the voice again:

My children are here—what a great joy!
Just what I'd hoped for, a girl and a boy!
Bring them to me, my beautiful fog.
Bring them to me and their memory I'll jog.
Answer my riddle or the fog it will fly—

Answer my riddle or you surely will die.

Even though we knew the answers, we were so scared we could hardly talk. The fog, the blue light, that awful voice made me panic so much I was afraid I'd forget the answers.

It's time, my children, to give me your
    answers
Tell me true, for there'll be no more chances.
Tell me the ship's name where I was
    stored in the hold.

"It was the whaleship *Joseph Starbuck*," Ben screamed.

"Tell me my captain who was careless yet bold," the sea chest bellowed.

"Your captain was Ichabod Paddack," I cried.

"How many tails were viewed on my trip?

How many whales met their end by my ship?" the voice demanded.

"You saw 177 whales and..." I stopped short. I couldn't remember for sure how many whales had been caught. Was it 55, 57 or 56? If I answered wrong, we were dead. The fog that was holding us would drag us into the sea chest, choke the life out of us and then get Grandma and Grandpa. "Ben, I can't remember!" I screamed. The voice let loose a tremendous tormenting laugh.

Then, calmly and confidently, I heard Ben say, "Your ship caught 56 whales."

Silence. The laughing stopped. The blue light flickered and the fog was suddenly being sucked back into the sea chest. The furniture and paintings in the attic began to take shape again. Then the last wisp of mist was back in the box, the lid slammed shut and the key from the museum popped out of the lock onto the floor.

CHAPTER
15

Ben and I just stared at the key. We couldn't believe that our nightmare was over. The attic was quiet and everything was back to normal. Ben bent down to pick up the key. And then we noticed the top of the sea chest. The riddle was gone. New words were carved there in its place.

This is the sea chest of
Ichabod Paddack
Captain of the whaleship *Joseph Starbuck,*
which met its fate in the fog off
the island of Nantucket.
177 whales were sighted and
56 captured on our final voyage.
Home and at peace at last.

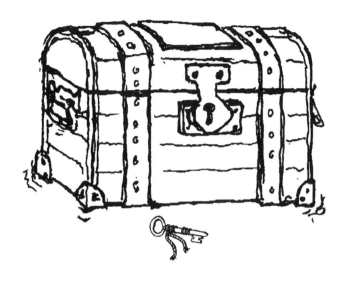

"Sarah and Ben, are you up there?" Grandma's voice woke us from our trance. "The sky is clearing and I've put together a picnic so we can go out to Madaket, have supper, and watch the sunset. Put on your sweatshirts and let's hit the road."

We didn't say a word all the way to the beach. Once there, we walked along the ocean and thought of Ichabod Paddack and his ship breaking up in the fog and the waves. He was probably as scared in the fog as we'd been.

As the sun set in the ocean and the colors filled the sky, Grandma, Grandpa, Rusty, Ben, and I cuddled together to stay warm. When the colors had started to fade, Grandma said, "There's quite a chill in the air. I sure hope the fog doesn't roll in tonight."

I quickly caught the look in Ben's eye and together we chimed, "So do we, Grandma, So...do...we!"

Watch for another
spooky tale from
Nantucket!
Here's a preview from
Warren Hussey Bouton's
The Ghost on
Main Street...

Dinnertime with Grandma and Grandpa was always an event. Not only was Grandma one of the best cooks on the island, but there was plenty of lively conversation to go along with the wonderful food. Tonight we feasted on spaghetti and the best garlic bread you ever tasted. Ben was full of stories of his baseball triumphs, from the six scoreless innings he'd pitched in a Little League playoff to the time when he was a catcher and threw two runners out in one game. Grandma caught us up on the changes around the island and Grandpa grumbled about all the work he'd been doing around the house. Whenever I got a chance to squeeze into the conversation I shared stories of my singing and acting in the latest musical at school.

When dinner was over and the dishes were cleared, washed, and put away we all moved into the living room. Ben and Grandpa started a game of checkers. Of course, before Ben knew what was happening Grandpa was beating him and my dear little brother was whining like crazy. Grandma and I spent the time enjoying each other's company until I looked up and noticed a strange picture on the wall. I'm sure it had been there forever, but I guess I just never really saw it before. It was an old picture of a teenage boy who looked very sad. "Who's that, Grandma?" I asked. "Why is he so sad?"

Looking up, Grandma said, "Oh, that's Cyrus, one of your ancestors. His family lived in this house back in the 1800's. That picture was painted shortly before he died."

"Why did he die, Grandma?" I wondered aloud.

"They say he died of a broken heart. Cyrus was a seaman on a whaling ship. While he was out on one of those three-year trips to the Pacific, the girl he loved was killed in the Great Fire of Nantucket. That was sometime in the mid 1800's. When his ship returned and Cyrus learned that she was gone, he never left this house again... alive."

The night wore on. Ben was trounced at checkers time and again by Grandpa. Ben just never knew when enough was enough. Grandma kept knitting and I tried to read, but I just couldn't get young Cyrus out of my head. He looked so unhappy! Even after I went to bed his sad eyes haunted me. I wondered if the room I was staying in had been his. After a long time I began to drift peacefully off to sleep, but suddenly, I heard something. It sounded like footsteps out in the hallway. I just knew it was my annoying brother trying to scare me. I turned on my light and shouted "Okay, Ben, you can stop now. I know it's you and you want me to scream and carry on—but it's not going to work tonight. I've lived with you long enough to know that you're trying to scare me!" Ben usually started to laugh as soon as I caught him at one his tricks. But there was no answer, and the footsteps came closer and closer to my door and then stopped. Quickly, I jumped out of bed and ran to try to catch Ben as I opened the door...but no one was there! The hall was empty. There was nothing but shadows and my own fears.

Closing my bedroom door behind me, I slowly moved back to my bed. I knew I had heard someone out there. If it wasn't Ben, who could it be? I turned off my light and as I settled back into bed I began to feel a gentle, sad presence in the darkness. I tried to pretend that it was just my imagination, but it felt so real. As I lay there, I remembered Cyrus again. I couldn't get him out of my head. It was spooky. And wasn't the last time that I felt something spooky on this trip.